# ALF ™
# A DAY AT THE FAIR

**Written by Johnson Hill**
**Illustrated by Eldon Doty**
**Cover by Ken Kimmelman**

CHECKERBOARD PRESS ✦ NEW YORK

ALF, the furry alien who lived with the Tanner family, came into the kitchen one morning.

"Guess what, ALF!" said Kate. "Today is Brian's birthday. I'm giving him this record."

"This is what I'm giving him," said Willie, bouncing a gleaming new basketball on the table.

"Well, I knitted a sweater for him," said Lynn. "I hope it fits."

"Yo! We have a problem," said ALF. "I don't have a present for Brian. Where can I get one?"

"Oh, ALF, I'm sorry," said Willie. "We were busy thinking about our presents for Brian. We forgot to ask you what you wanted to give him. I hope you don't feel too bad."

"Hey, no problem," answered ALF gloomily.

"Poor ALF!" sighed Lynn. "I know what! Why don't we take him with us to the fair this afternoon?"

"Whoa!" said Willie. "What will people think when they see him?"

"Well," said Kate, "we'll just have to disguise him carefully, that's all."

"Great! I feel better already," said ALF. "Let's eat!"

ALF and the Tanners arrived at the fairground. ALF and Brian were excited by all the sights and sounds.

Willie gave Brian and ALF each a dollar to spend.

"And what does a dollar buy these days?" ALF complained to himself.

A blimp floated gracefully overhead. ALF watched it for a while.

When he stopped watching the blimp, he looked around. He was alone. The Tanners were nowhere in sight!

"Yikes!" ALF said bravely. "I'm on my own." But he looked around anyway, hoping to see one of the Tanners pop out of the crowd.

Suddenly ALF had an idea. "I can use my dollar to win a present for Brian!"

So ALF tossed rings to win a prize.
Next he threw darts.
Then he aimed at bottles.

But he didn't win anything.
"These games are all for people
with five fingers," he grumbled.

ALF heard someone yelling at him. A big man stood by a strange machine. He pointed to ALF.

"Hurry, hurry, hurry! Win the grand prize! Test your strength!"

"Step right up, fella," he said to ALF. "All you have to do is hit this strength machine with the mallet and ring the bell. Then you win a <u>fabulous</u> prize!"

ALF stepped up to the machine. People quickly gathered around to watch. "There goes another fool," someone muttered.

ALF grabbed the mallet, raised it over his head, and brought it down with a mighty blow! And the machine's bell rang loudly!

Everyone in the crowd looked surprised. "It was nothing," said ALF modestly. "All those pushups I did on Melmac paid off."

ALF won an enormous teddy bear!
"Oh, boy. Brian will really like this,"
he said, clutching the bear.

ALF wandered through the fairground, looking for the Tanners. They were nowhere to be found.

Finally he decided to wait by the ring-toss booth, where he had last seen them.

ALF was tired. He sat down next to the booth and fell asleep.

A little girl was tossing rings. She won a prize.
"Choose your own," said the man who ran the booth.
The girl looked around and saw ALF. "I want that one!" she exclaimed.
"Sure, miss," said the man.

ALF woke up suddenly. Someone was hugging him. Someone was trying to pick him up!

"Yo!" ALF shook himself. The little girl screeched in surprise.

ALF stared at her. "Hey!" he said happily. "You remind me of someone I knew back on Melmac!"

The girl's father started to argue with the man in the booth.
The man in the booth was looking <u>very</u> oddly at the little alien.
"Uh-oh!" thought ALF. "Should I scoot, or what?"
Then just in the nick of time, ALF heard a welcome sound . . .

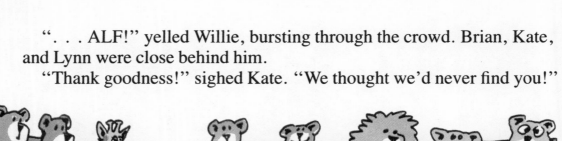

". . . ALF!" yelled Willie, bursting through the crowd. Brian, Kate, and Lynn were close behind him.

"Thank goodness!" sighed Kate. "We thought we'd never find you!"

ALF held out the teddy bear. "This is for you, old buddy," he said to Brian. "Happy birthday! Um, sorry I didn't have time to gift-wrap it."

"Gee, thanks!" said Brian. "I always wanted a bear this big!"

"Whew. I got hot and tired looking for you," said Lynn. "Let's all go cool off on one of the rides."

"Great," said Willie. How about the merry-go-round or the Ferris wheel? ALF, what would you like to do?"